Refried Dreams

PRAISE FOR *STORYSHARES*

"One of the brightest innovators and game-changers in the education industry."
– Forbes

"Your success in applying research-validated practices to promote literacy serves as a valuable model for other organizations seeking to create evidence-based literacy programs."
- Library of Congress

"We need powerful social and educational innovation, and Storyshares is breaking new ground. The organization addresses critical problems facing our students and teachers. I am excited about the strategies it brings to the collective work of making sure every student has an equal chance in life."
– Teach For America

"Around the world, this is one of the up-and-coming trailblazers changing the landscape of literacy and education."
- International Literacy Association

"It's the perfect idea. There's really nothing like this. I mean wow, this will be a wonderful experience for young people."   - Andrea Davis Pinkney, Executive Director, Scholastic

"Reading for meaning opens opportunities for a lifetime of learning. Providing emerging readers with engaging texts that are designed to offer both challenges and support for each individual will improve their lives for years to come. Storyshares is a wonderful start."
- David Rose, Co-founder of CAST & UDL

Refried Dreams

Sarah Haas

STORYSHARES

Story Share, Inc.
New York. Boston. Philadelphia

Storyshares
Story Share, Inc.
24 N. Bryn Mawr Avenue #340
Bryn Mawr, PA 19010-3304
www.storyshares.org

Inspiring reading with a new kind of book.

Interest Level: High School
Grade Level Equivalent: 3.7

9781642613131

Book design by Storyshares

Printed in the United States of America

Storyshares Presents

1

My future smelled as smooth as raspberry vanilla with a hint of almond. Of course, the employment application for Koala Gelato just smelled dry and inky. Still, it felt like fame and fortune in my hands.

"Did you just *smell* that application?" Clara asked, squinting one eye in disdain. Clara, the cashier, always kept her nails blue. I bought gelato-rich italian ice cream from her at least twice a week. But now, elegant Clara thought I was weird for smelling paper.

I was determined that my first job would be at this sleek gelato shop. And now, one of its employees already thought I was weird. *Great.*

"Yes," I said. "Haven't you ever smelled something because it was exciting or important? Like your first driver's license? Or the newest book in your favorite series? Or your locker on the first day of school?"

"No. Definitely not . . . Melanie Parson," she said, reading my name off the application.

Now she thinks I am even weirder! Surely, she would tell her boss which girl was the freak. *Why do I have the gift of always saying the wrong thing?*

"Oh. Umm. I was just trying to say that I'm excited about this application because I believe in your company."

"Yeah. The lazy Mexicans across the food court believe in their company, too. And it hasn't gotten *them* very far."

Forget about racist Clara, I told myself. *She isn't the one who hires people.* Soon, I would be wearing a thin gray apron with blue trim. I would build cookie sculptures of the Leaning Tower of Pisa with honey flavored ice cream. The mall would hum and shuffle all around me as I watched from the center of the food court. They would pay me to chat with shoppers and smile at boys.

A cute boy stood behind me in line right then, actually. I practiced a smile on him as I turned to go.

"Do you seriously smell your locker?!" he smirked.

2

My future smelled as stale as cold fries and old salsa.

I stopped by Koala Gelato to ask about my application for the seventh time. First, I spent $4.16 on a medium-sized scoop of coconut breeze. Then, the manager told me they had no openings.

Actually, he asked me to repeat my name, then glanced at a note on my application. *Then* he told me that they had no openings. As if to say that they might have had an opening if I were someone else.

I couldn't accept defeat. This was my dream! Everybody's first job had to be food service. It was like a rite of passage. But Koala Gelato made the food court look stylish and cool. The teen employees there acted like they had already started careers and just did school on the side.

One day, I planned to be an engineer or an architect. For now, I was going to work at Koala Gelato. I was sure of it. I would do whatever it took to work there: apply again, beg the manager . . . anything. Maybe they'd need more workers in a few months.

My mom had never tried gelato, so she didn't understand my passion. She came home the next evening with an application for Mexicandy America, the restaurant that was trying to combine Mexican food with desserts and burgers. It was failing at all three.

"You wanted to work in the food court, right?" Mom said. "Mexicandy America is right across from Koala Gelato! You could get ice cream on your breaks."

"Mom. That place is *revolting.*"

"You don't have to like the food to work there, Melanie. The way to get a job is by applying to lots of places. This is just one of the many jobs you can apply for."

"That place gives me the creeps. I'd rather not have a job than work there."

Mom pointed at the bills clamped to the refrigerator. "You know that's not an option, honey. I'm sorry, but that's how it is for us."

Ten months ago, Mom went to urgent care feeling lightheaded and short of breath. The next thing I knew, I was in the hospital waiting room while Mom had heart surgery. She was in the hospital for five days. I went home to sleep because she made me. I went to school two of those days because she made me. Otherwise, I didn't leave her room.

I didn't cry, not once. I also didn't eat anything other than Doritos that whole week. Some people leak grief out of their eyes. They think they can drain it out of their system. I shoved mine into my mouth and tried to crush it up into microscopic cheese dust.

Everybody told us afterward that they were so thankful Mom made it. No one was thankful enough to help pay the hospital bills. Those bills put all the stress that the doctors had tried to suck out of Mom's veins right back in. We'd been keeping up with living expenses before the surgery but just barely. Mom needed help. That meant I needed a job. I didn't mind. At least, not until now. Not until it came to *this*.

I stopped complaining to Mom, but I also didn't surrender. Hutson County wasn't exactly overflowing with strip malls or major chains, but it had enough businesses that I knew I could get a job somewhere else. I'd sell clothes, scan groceries, or even pick up dog poop. Anything that offered a little more social standing than Mexicandy America.

3

The weeks ticked by, and Mom was right. No one was hiring.

"We just filled our opening last week," one manager said.

Another shoved my application under the counter. He never took his eyes off the computer screen in front of him. "Thanks so much. We'll give you a call," he muttered.

Forget about that liar, I told myself. *He smelled like wet laundry anyway.*

"Sorry," said an older woman. "It's nothing personal, hon."

I stepped up my game for the next few weeks. I practiced my brightest smile in the bathroom mirror. I switched my Dr. Who hoodie for an Old Navy polo. Nothing said *hire me* like wearing a square of industrial carpet topped with a man's collar. For some reason, that still didn't work. I was reaching the end of my list.

Mom was nagging. Don't get me wrong, she didn't want to make me work, but we needed the money. We both knew it.

One morning, I found the Mexicandy America application on the kitchen table. It was already filled out in Mom's bubbly handwriting. A Post-it note marked the signature line. I stood over it, uncertain.

"Drop you off after school today?" she asked. Her eyes added, *Please?*

What could I do? I'd tried my way, and I'd lost.

I still didn't think it was really going to happen, but I had been defeated. So I handed my application to the man behind the register at Mexicandy America. Still, I figured they wouldn't hire me because I was too white and too blonde. Everyone who worked there was Mexican, not to mention male.

Instead, the manager didn't even read my paperwork. He said he would interview me. I thought he meant in a day or next week, but he meant right then at the side of the counter.

"Do you work hard?" he asked. *José*, his nametag said. *Owner.*

"I don't actually know. I've never had a job before."

"You *will* work hard," José said. "Okay then. Are you friendly with customers?"

"I think so. I mean sometimes I get annoyed or blurt out dumb things, like now."

"You *will* be friendly with customers. All the time."

Two out of two answers wrong. I didn't actually want the job, so I wasn't worried.

"Can you start tomorrow?" José asked.

A guy standing by the back leaned out and yelled something in Spanish. I didn't speak Spanish. That was another reason I shouldn't work there. I recognized one word from Dora the Explorer: *bienvenidos.* Welcome. He wore an apron the color of hot peppers. His hair was gelled up into a triangle in the middle of his head.

I was about to dazzle him with my stunning Spanish vocabulary: *gracias*. But then he chucked a long wooden spoon at me. I tried to catch it. Instead, I knocked it into my nose.

I blushed and turned to leave. This place was downright abusive. Then I saw Mom strolling into the food court to pick me up. She saw that I was talking to the manager. She threw on a cheesy grin and a double thumbs-up. Then she ducked around the corner to wait.

Dang it, I couldn't do this to her. What could I do? Lie to her and pretend I didn't get the job? *Sorry, Mom. I'd rather you died of a heart attack than help pay for your recovery. See, I just dont want to spread pico de gallo on hamburger buns. Nothing personal.*

"Yeah, I can start tomorrow." Like I said, I always gave the wrong answer.

I threw the spoon back at the rude cook. It missed him and flew into a chunk of metal above the grill. The cook rolled his eyes. José muttered a string of words that I assumed were curses. I glanced at Koala Gelato across the hall. Clara had her hands over her ears and a perfect-for-Instagram pout on her face.

Fries and salsa with a burnt tortilla cookie on the side. *Great.*

4

José turned out to be better at interviewing than he was at training. On my first day, he handed me an apron the color of old guacamole and sat me down in front of a computer. Then, I watched a forty-minute animation about what to do in the case of a bomb threat.

I paid more attention to the strange voices in the kitchen, yipping and yelling in endlessly confusing Spanish. I think they even laughed in Spanish. Loneliness found me in that moment. I would never know my coworkers, never laugh with them or at them. Most of them were teenage guys, perfect candidates for friends or an awkward prom date. Instead, they would always belong to themselves while I stood alone with my English.

Near the end of the video, a skinny cook poked his head in the door and laughed at my solemn white face. Then he slipped back to his jungle of spatulas. After the video, José put me at the cash register without any explanation.

"I'll have a large refried burger with extra sour cream," said a wiry woman. Both the large burger and I could have crawled into her purse. "But no ketchup. And make that a meal, but with rice instead of fries and a medium jalapeño shake. To go."

Forty tiny buttons glowed on the screen in a neon rainbow. I couldn't read any of them; the words were abbreviated to three or four letters. Which one was the refried burger? Was it the one that began with an *r* or a *b*? The woman sighed.

"José!" I squeaked. "José! Where's the refried burger?"

José must have been in the back office, hiding from my disasters up front. I guess desperation sounds the same in every language because Triangle-Head Boy stomped up and thumbed a button. He turned to go, but I latched onto his elbow. "Wait! It needs extra ketchup . . . how do I add that?"

"No ketchup and extra sour cream," the woman said, annoyed.

The cook entered her order all over again, his fingers whirling over the buttons so fast I could hardly see what he was punching. "That's how. Easy, no?" he said to me.

"No! Not really."

He spread his hands. "You learn." He headed back to the kitchen to re-fry her order. I glanced at his nametag as he brushed past me: Raúl.

I didn't really want to learn. I was just biding time here until I landed a better job. The clock said I had two hours and forty-two minutes before I could go home and wash away the stink of minimum wage.

Refried Dreams

5

Raúl came back again half an hour later. He spoke Spanish to me, but I didn't understand.

"Look, Rawl, I don't know Spanish, so . . ."

"Rrraúl. *Mi nombre es . . .* my name is Rrraúl."

"Uh, Rahool, then. Sorry. Like I said, I don't know Spanish. I can't even say your name right. You put little frills and stuff on your 'R.' It sounds awesome, really, it does, but my tongue isn't that fancy. This really isn't the job for me. I don't fit in here." I pointed at my arm and then his. "I know you guys probably don't want me here either, so I'm going to find a new job soon, okay? I'll just get out of everybody's way, and we'll all be happier."

Raúl had gone still. Maybe I'd struck a nerve, but I was curious now, so I kept going. "Are *you* happy here?" I asked him. "Is this what you want?"

"You learn?" He motioned toward the register. He hadn't understood a word I said. "Not yet," I told him. "No one will train me."

He stepped forward and started clicking on the screen, continuing to speak to me in Spanish. As soon as I got home, I was going to Google translate the phrase, "I don't speak Spanish," and safety-pin it to my uniform. This guy just didn't take a hint.

Ves? Burger. *Aquí*. Here. He pointed to one of the buttons. He was trying to teach me. "*Gracias*. But, um, I think I'll wait for José to teach me. José," I pointed to the screen and then myself. "José will teach me." *At least José speaks English.*

Raúl nodded slowly and exhaled through his mouth before babbling in Spanish again. I threw my hands up in a helpless shrug. This was why I needed José to teach me. I had no idea what Raúl was going on about.

Donde pertenecemos, no? En el fondo. He walked away, mad about who knows what.

Two hours and four minutes until I was done with the shift. And, by my calculations, seven applications, two interviews, and one lucky call until I was done with the job.

Refried Dreams

6

My first weeks were stressful and silent. I was always self-conscious. I felt scared that Clara scorned my tacky orange visor from across the food court, scared that the Spanish words frying and sizzling through the kitchen were about me.

I tried to turn off the fear. But it was true that sometimes I caught my coworkers watching me, grinning. I didn't buy gelato anymore. I was embarrassed enough without talking to Clara.

With time, I learned the cash register system, more out of boredom than effort. I gave myself a C average on taking orders correctly. That was my mom's grade standard: nothing below seventy percent. If the kind people at the ACT board gave bonus points for punching in buttons right, I'd be well on my way to Harvard by now. And if the number of applications I'd turned in counted for anything, I was well on my way *out* of Mexicandy America.

My biggest weakness was that I still had the awful habit of replying wrong every time a customer lured me into small talk. For example, when one man asked if I was in school, I answered, "No, I'm at work."

Another time, a woman asked how my mom was doing. I told her that I didn't recognize her. It turned out that she had been our neighbor until six months ago, and she was a little offended. José bumped her medium rice pudding up to a large for free. Then, he pulled me aside.

"We're always friendly to the customer here, remember? Always. But you give them that scared look on your face. Then, you say strange things, and they feel unwelcome here."

"I'm sorry, José. I don't always know what to say. I guess I'm just bad with people."

"You're not bad with people. You're just not good with them. Be friendly to the customers," he said again.

Meanwhile, the cooks and I came to an understanding in the form of a two-fingered salute. One afternoon when I arrived for my shift, I greeted the tall cook with a lazy salute. Apparently, it was the funniest signal he'd ever seen.

I should have been annoyed and insecure about the whole thing. For some reason, I wasn't anymore. Maybe I'd stopped caring. Maybe it was a relief to have something in common with the cooks. Now they all saluted me when I came in. I saluted back, and they grinned. Raúl put an extra flair on his. Sometimes he stood stiff-kneed like a nutcracker. Other times, he looped his hand in the air like he was twirling a ballerina. I chucked spoons, wooden *and* metal at him, but I also laughed.

That was all, though. We might act out a joke or two with our hands and facial expressions. Then it was back to work. It was easy enough for them. The guys could grill, scrub, and stock while chattering. I was alone.

Refried Dreams

7

For a while, I talked to myself or to them in English. After all, it wasn't like they understood me anyway.

"I don't get it," I said. "You guys are a lot cooler than I thought. If you learned English, you could do anything you wanted." They must have heard me because a few of them gave me weird looks. *Got it.* Talking to yourself must be the universal sign of insanity.

After that, I just took orders and watched the clock. I tried to keep quiet and avoid extra conversation with customers. When business was slow, I doodled on napkins.

I was trying to draw a Viking helmet on top of a skirted stick figure one evening when Mom walked up to the counter forty minutes early. "Hey! I'm not off yet," I said.

"I know. I want to try your food here. Today, I'm a customer first and a driver second."

"Uhh, Mom, we don't have anything you can eat." It probably wasn't wise for anyone to eat the food sold at Mexicandy America. That was especially true for Mom. Her doctors had her on a super-strict, heart-healthy diet. At home, I had to choose between grazing in a pasture with Mom or excusing myself to microwave pizza rolls.

"I know it's fast food," she said, "but I haven't had any sugar for two weeks to prepare for this." Dang, she was all in. I didn't really know why. Surely motherly love was no match for the nuclear reaction that she was about to swallow. "What do you suggest?"

"Um, there's not really anything."

Disculpe, bonita. Raúl had slipped up to my side. *Tu mama?* he asked.

Hey! I understood what he meant!

"Yeah," I said. "This is my mom."

He turned his attention to her. "We cook," he said. "You no pay. Okay?"

"Oh, thank you!" she said, "but that's not necessary. I want to support the business where Melanie works."

"Familia no pay." Raúl ended the matter with a polite smile and then barked orders at the kitchen crew. I leaned over to see which trainwreck they were making her. I didn't recognize the dish as anything on the menu. One of them was slicing fresh tomatoes. I didn't know we had any fresh tomatoes. And they were using the skillet instead of the microwave.

Raúl brought it out to Mom himself.

"This smells amazing! I can't wait to try it," she said, and he smiled. She looked really happy as she carried her tray to a nearby table. I turned back to face Raúl. I was grateful for the weird way he was acting. I hadn't expected this from him.

Maybe because I wanted so badly to say something nice, I blurted out the opposite. "We're not poor," I lied.

"I'm not illegal," Raúl said.

'What?" *How did that even come up?* I never said anything like that.

Raúl tapped his head twice. "You have it *aqui . . .* here. Okay? I'm not." He didn't make a dramatic exit to the back this time. He might as well have because it was quiet after that. Things just went better for me whenever I kept my mouth shut.

First, Raúl covered Mom's meal and cooked for her. Then, he went off on me about something I never said. I wasn't sure if we were friends now or enemies. We were, at least, soldiers. Because when Mom came back to thank the guys for a great meal, every single one of the cooks saluted her. Raúl led them like a general.

8

When I closed my eyes, two things happened. First, I saw myself sitting on the sofa with Mom and telling her that I had forty thousand dollars. Granted, I didn't know how I was going to get that forty thousand. Maybe winning nationals at the robotics competition or working at a place that paid twenty times what I made here. Maybe I'd impress a customer who turned out to be the CEO of a fancy perfume company looking for a young life to change.

However it would happen, I could see it just the same: Mom would be scrolling on her phone and casually mm-hmming until I dropped the number. Then she would gasp, ask if I was sure, start crying, and hug me. She'd tell me I didn't have to use it all on her bills and that I should save it for my future.

"No, Mom," I would reply. "My future starts here, with you."

The second thing I'd see is José yelling at me to wake up and watch the counter.

Except he yelled a little nicer than usual today. He'd brought his toddler daughter, and the kid mellowed him out fairly well. Even José's baby knew more Spanish than I did. She yammered all her little words at the cooks, words like *el gato, caramelas, la barba del gigante.* She spoke English, too . . . A toddler had picked up two languages, but I couldn't! "Yellow hair! *Bonita!*" she said, pointing at me.

José bounced her in his arms and turned to me. "She's calling you."

"Do I want to know?" I cut in. I had heard that word before: *bonita.* I was sure it meant dumb, nerdy, lazy, or spoiled white girl. The cooks said it all the time.

He chuckled. "Melanie, you're as insecure as Raúl, you know that?"

Raúl, insecure? Hardly.

"*Bonita* means pretty. I thought you knew that. It's your nickname here."

A compliment?! Shocked, I dropped the salsa slushee I had been holding. No one ever called me pretty. On the days when I put a little extra effort in, people told me that I looked nice or fine. They didn't drag the word out and make it musical, either. They said it short and clipped, like that was all the time they were going to waste on the matter.

"Sorry!" I cried, kneeling in the red-orange slush.

"C'mon, you clumsy kid!" said the customer. "I'm in a rush."

"Sorry, ma'am," José said on my behalf. "I'll make you a new one. Let me just take Cici to the back room first, yes?" Before he did, he leaned over me and added, "I hope you're not offended. *Bonita* is a respectful word, not a trashy one."

"If they meant respect, they could help me clean this up," I mumbled.

Still, I felt pretty. I felt like I could do anything. I probably didn't *look* pretty at the moment, since I was on my knees crying joyfully into a puddle of slushee. But when Cici looked at me, she saw an angel with golden hair. That was all I needed.

"I'm supposed to be at work in ten minutes," the customer snapped. "I should've just paid the extra for a gelato."

Suddenly, I felt determined to beat Koala Gelato. I wasn't worthless. I was *pretty*. I wasn't good at this gig, not yet, but I was *going* to be. Never again would someone regret choosing my dessert over Clara's.

I, the so-called clumsy kid, and they, the so-called lazy Mexicans . . . *we*, the stupid lower class and fast-food failures, were about to outsell the most popular food stand in the mall.

9

Melanie Parsons and the Hispanic chefs versus Clara and the Italian ice cream squad! It would be a duel of desserts! Let the losers surrender the food court!

Koala had the head start, but our middle name was literally candy. Starting now, we would be *good* at making candy. Every sweet tooth in the city would crave us, even if they could afford gelato. My uniform would smell less like the green sludge at the bottom of trash bags and more like sugarplums.

Meanwhile, the cooks were pelting one another with cheese chunks. We had a long way to go.

"Hola!" I cried, dumbly waving as if I had never seen them before. In a way, I hadn't. I still couldn't keep their names all straight—the thin one, the big-bearded one, the one who always wore sandals. Carlos, Pablo, Victor . . . and Julio? There was also Anibal and Disael, however you pronounced *that.*

"Hola," the skinny one smiled. "*Maylanie.*"

"Our food is bad," I said. "The coffee kidney bean casserole is bad. The nugget burritos are bad. Making a *tres leches* cake by pouring skim milk, chocolate milk, and strawberry milk over yellow cake? Very bad." I swept my hand up to the menu board over my head. "All of our food is bad. Everything. Bad."

They all nodded. "*Si.* The food is bad."

The short one held the cheese up to his mouth and then stuck his tongue out, chucking it across the kitchen to show that he did not eat anything from Mexicandy America. "José . . . it is his menu, no? He pays, so we cook his menu."

"José likes people to come here and buy food. People don't like the food, so soon José will have no money to pay us with," I said. "We have to make something new." They stared at me. They did not understand.

New, new, what's the universal sign for *new?* We have to cook good food. Different food. Food *you* like."

They were all talking at one another, leaving me alone to brainstorm a way to save the restaurant.

10

I was so stressed that I started talking to myself. Every last person in the mall already thought I was a freak, so I might as well keep the image up.

"We're going out of business unless we start cooking better food," I said, "and dang it, I need the paycheck." There was nothing I could do about it.

These guys just put frozen beans in microwaves, poured them over French fries, and called it good.

The Spanish stopped. One of the guys turned to me and said in English, "I can cook. Disael, Pablo, Carlos . . . they can cook, too."

"You understood me?" I squeaked.

The skinny one answered, *Por supuesto*, which meant absolutely nothing to me.

"Yes," Raúl cut in. He clapped the skinny one on the back. Then he turned to me. "Yes, we understand English," he said slowly. "It's just hard to say, and you no listen."

Huh. So they could understand me all along, but I just hadn't bothered trying to talk to them. I thought language was binary: you either knew English or you didn't, and that was all. I thought Mexican food and American food didn't go together. Come to think of it, I didn't think Mexican and American *anything* went together. But these guys understood me. Now *I* just needed to learn how to understand *them*.

First, the food problem. We needed fresh recipes and a fine hand. I was skeptical.

Escuchame, Raúl was saying. "We are talking food. Plans. We can cook."

"I know you guys do your best here, but we need a chef. A professional cook. New recipes."

Nunca me escuchas! Raúl suddenly yelled. He threw a spoon angrily, harder than I'd seen him throw before. I stepped back and bit my lower lip. I'd never seen Raúl like this.

Then he started laughing just as hard. "*Bonita*, this time, listen. Learn, okay? Remember when your *mama* came? We cook different food for her. We. Can. Cook."

"Yeah, actually, she talked about that a lot. She said she didn't know what you guys made for her, but whatever it was, it was amazing. I just hadn't believed her at the time. I figured she was being nice."

"I know." He grinned. "You are up here at the counter for a reason."

"Hey!"

"You are the one who reminds us to be proud of the *restaurante*. Not just come, do job, go home. You remind us to care. To dream. So, *bonita, gracias*."

And I swear he handed me that spoon as gently as if it were a rose.

Refried Dreams

11

So I jumped on my horse and yelled, "Chaaaarge!" We all rushed to the battlefield in a fury of family recipes and charades. I abandoned the register and stood with them for the first time. I figured out which one was Pablo, Carlos, and Anibal. I doodled recipe formulas on the insides of sandwich wrappers. José showed up on his day off, caught us red-handed, and gave his approval. He even promised us a raise if our plans worked.

"Why don't you say things like this more often, Melanie?" he asked. "Instead of all those weird comments. This is what I hired you for!"

Disael sizzled fat chorizo sausage speckled with spices on the grill. Then he baptized it in pure American glory: an outer roll of bacon. Julio stirred up a melting pot of broth, shredded chicken, corn, cilantro, lime juice, sour cream, and every kind of cheese we had on hand. Pablo said he could sprinkle hot chili peppers and onions on top of a pork chop. He wasn't going to waste his time until we got higher-quality meat, though. At least, I think that's what he said.

Raúl was directing the whole thing. He told everyone else when it was their turn on the grill or where extra ingredients were stashed. He made me stand at his side so he could teach me as he plastered corn flakes and honey onto balls of cinnamon ice cream. I'd come full circle here, making fried ice cream now instead of scooping gelato. While we worked, he made me repeat Spanish words after him.

"First word: *bonita. Bonita* is pretty."

"I know that one already."

"Oh, you know already that you are *bonita*, huh?" he laughed. Making fried ice cream was easier than it looked. Maybe because Raúl guided my fingers every time I paused.

"That's not what I meant! I just know the definition. That's all." *Dang it, I always manage to say the wrong—*

He wasn't listening. "Next: *orgullosa*. It is, uh, girl who thinks big about yourself."

"Proud?"

"Yes! Proud. *Bonita y orgullosa*. Say it."

"I am not *bonita y oh-goo-yo-sa!*"

"Muy bien!" Somehow, he'd gotten a smudge of ice cream on his cheek. It brushed against his eyelashes when he smiled. "Next: *Cuchara.*

"Cuchara. What does *cuchara* mean?"

Raúl held up a spoon and waved it just out of reach.

12

Clara stood in front of the counter and called my name.

All these months, I'd been trying to ignore her. But I couldn't stop wondering: did she remember me? Did she scorn me every time I clocked in and set up camp beneath our blazing orange and yellow menu? Or maybe she had forgotten me by now. After all, she'd only been there five of the eight times I'd asked for a job at Koala Gelato. Which would be worse: to be the target of her insults or to be so unnoticeable that she'd forgotten my existence altogether?

I wanted to be Clara. I wanted to delicately down a scoop of raspberry kale gelato made with almond milk every shift and still look good in my work clothes. I wanted Clara to grin at me with an inside joke more sophisticated than Raúl's and my awkward slapstick. I just wanted her to approve of me.

"Melanie Parson!"

I jumped up so quickly that my elbow smashed the ice cream ball off the counter and onto Raúl's side, but I didn't slow down to apologize. I was in front of that register in two seconds, smiling a little too big and reaching under the counter for some napkins to wipe up my elbow.

"Clara! Hi! What can I get you? We have, um, fried ice cream today. That would be perfect for you! I think you would love it. Raúl, can you make a new . . ."

"I'm not here to order anything from this place," Clara said. "I only eat organic. I came to offer you a job."

I stopped scrubbing at my elbow and gasped. No way. "You did?"

"Well, I'm not technically a manager, but Randy is sick today. He asked me to come hunt you down." She cringed at something behind me.

I turned to see Victor and Disael flipping pepperonis at each other. Anibal commentated their battle like it was the World Cup, and Pablo laughed so loud I couldn't hear the meat frying anymore. Raúl, on the other hand, was just staring at us with his hands at his sides and ice cream dripping down like tears from his apron, listening to every word.

I guess they did look pretty bad from a distance. People worth getting to know generally do.

"I thought you didn't want me," I told Clara. "I asked eight times."

"Business isn't personal, kid," she said, as if we weren't in the same grade. "We didn't have a lot of openings then. A few, but we had the luxury to be a little more selective. Anyway, a lot of people have left us the past few weeks."

If they fired workers at Koala Gelato for bad attitude, how had Clara survived?

"You don't need to know all this," she continued. "Point is: we're desperate, and that's why were giving you a shot. You've retained employment . . . kept *this* job, at least for a few months now. So, Randy figures you must be able to take an order."

"Wow," I said. "Thank you. I can take an order in my sleep! And I already know the entire Koala Gelato menu. I'll be your best employee. I can bring in more business, too! I'm designing some major business changes at Mexicandy America right now. We're really fixing this place up, you know? Building something new."

Clara flicked her eyes at the kitchen behind me and raised one eyebrow. "We don't need a makeover," she said. "We just need someone to punch numbers. Starting salary is $8.25 an hour. Here's Randys number if you have any questions." She tossed a business card on the counter. "You start Tuesday, six to ten."

"You mean, it's a done deal already? No interview?"

"Just show up, and it's yours. Don't be late because this opportunity won't come again. Trust me. It wasn't this easy for me, and I actually come from class."

Having done her duty, she turned to go, but I stopped her. "Clara? Can I ask you something?" She turned back. "I see you at school sometimes. I don't think you see me. You just live your life, you know? And I live mine. You don't seem like a bully, but every time I see you at the mall, you act like I did something horrible to you."

I was scared to ask the question. This was the wrong thing to say. Clara had just offered me my dream job. Her boss must have thought I was a hard worker. But a bad fairy cursed me at birth to ruin every human interaction that came my way, so out it came: "Why do you dislike me so much?"

Clara sighed and slumped her shoulders. "I don't dislike you," she said in a voice that suggested the opposite. "Honestly, you're just really weird, okay? You don't fit the Koala Gelato look. You don't even try. This place seems like a better fit for you. The people here are more . . . low-key. So I don't know why Randy's bringing you on but whatever. You won't ruin the business, and we don't have to be friends. So I don't care."

And she strutted back to her Koala castle.

13

I ran my thumb along the business card that Clara left behind. Suddenly, I realized that the kitchen was quiet. I could hear every drop of water boiling out of Julio's soup. When I turned around, all the guys were staring at me with empty, frozen faces. Raúl must have told them what he'd heard.

"Look, I'm sorry," I said.

"You work there now," Raúl said. It wasn't a question.

"It's nothing personal. You know I've been having fun here with you guys. But my mom . . . I never told you about my mom. And she . . ." It was too much. I needed a bag of Doritos fast, before I started crying in front of all of them.

"My mom and I need the money. That's a dollar more per hour than I make here. A dollar an hour! I don't really have a choice."

Pablo pointed back at the five different recipes now burning on various parts of the grill. "The new food. You said!"

"I know, but look, guys. You don't need me anymore. You're the cooks, not me. I don't even speak Spanish. I'm not good with customers. I guess you all heard what Clara said about me, so why do you want me? I'm weird. So, you'll be fine."

"You no listen to me, but you listen to her," said Raúl. "You believe her. I tell you that you bring us dreams. I didn't speak much English. I had shame about my English. Now I speak it. I try. And I feel *orgulloso,* proud, of who I am. I am proud to be Raúl. But you think that is *nada*, nothing. To make people want to be more."

"Okay, then. Let's say I gave you dreams. You have them now. You don't need me. You guys are already enough."

Raúl was talking faster now. His English became sloppier, but it also sounded a little more like him. "You ask me once what is my dream. If I am happy here. No. I was *aburrido*, not happy. And I have dreams, okay? I want to learn computers. But past weeks, I am happy here. Because . . . because . . ." he glanced sideways, took a deep breath, and met my eye again quickly. "Because of you."

Then nobody said anything. They just stood there and let the soup smolder. Finally, Pablo saluted me. Victor was next. Then they turned back to the food. The others followed their example, saluting me one by one. It used to be our rallying cry into battle. Now it was their way to bury a fallen comrade.

Dang it! This was just a minimum-wage job at a fast food restaurant that was on its way out of business, not a soap opera!

Everybody needed to calm down, including me.

Raúl was last. "If you need more *cucharas* there, tell me. I throw you one." He lifted his first two fingers to salute me, then brought them down to touch his lips.

14

I inhaled my glorious, *delicioso* present. I breathed
and breathed until my lungs almost popped. It was
Tuesday night, almost six o' clock. My life was about to
change, but not just my life, everyone's. I was so excited
that I cocked my visor sideways and leaned over the
counter. I wanted a front-row seat to watch the food
court whiff its future.

We all decided to sell churros as our first new food.
Everyone but me was an expert at frying the sticky dough

into long sticks of sugar. Churros perfectly fulfilled Mexicandy America's food style. They were a Mexican dish, a dessert, and had all the grease that American fast food could offer. I knew the guys didn't think I was a cook, but even I helped. I did my country proud when I dunked the hot churros into chocolate. I then welded M&Ms, Reeses Pieces, and crushed Oreos to the sides. Now *this* was engineering.

That wasn't even the best part. Deep frying the sticky blob produced an incredible smell. Even Mom's doctors would break their diets to get these churros in their mouths.

The scent was in my nose and hair. It spread out all over the cash register. It tiptoed into the air, past the square tables and under the chairs. It was cinnamon and sugar. It was rubies in a treasure chest. It was the perfume I imagined when I looked at maps of Europe.

Ah, the scent of those churros! It walked across the room to a circle of girls. They twisted their hair in its fashionable presence. It sat on the McDonalds counter and knocked its feet against the ledge. It filled tired janitors with old dreams they'd forgotten. And last of all, it told Clara that it did *not* want an application, thank you very much.

Clara's nostrils twitched. Then, her whole face twitched.

Something smelled *good*. That is, Mexicandy America smelled good. And it wasn't supposed to. And I, the awkward girl with boy hair, was saluting her in triumph instead. Raúl crept up behind me and shoved a spoon inside my orange visor. It looked like the plastic feathers stuck on top of a Native American chief's hair piece. I left it in and raised my head higher.

I cared. I cared about this weird little restaurant. I cared about its workers who knew that no matter what went wrong, it's better to laugh than cry. I cared about my mom. She taught me to put people first, always. The money would come around somehow.

Clara was right: business wasn't personal. Raúl was right, too: *familia* didn't pay. I didn't used to have a dad figure who sighed when I made his life complicated and mumbled awkward affections now and then. Or a gang of brothers who teased me exactly when I didn't want them to. But when I looked back across the kitchen, I knew that now I did.

Business wasn't personal, but *familia* wasn't business.

So I stayed at Mexicandy America. After all, I completed the team. The guys had the Mexican-American part down. They were pretty good at that blend. But *candy* was in the name, too. And I was the sweet one.

On second thought, I pulled the spoon out of my hat and hit Raúl.

"What's that smell?" I heard a kid say from in front of Koala. "I think I want to try it."

"Me too. Let's go," his friend agreed. The two drifted out of Clara's line. And then three more followed. And another. Just one kid remained at Koala Gelato.

I watched the loner trying to choose what to do. I could tell he was tempted by our yummy smell. On the other hand, the gelato girl was waving all of her blue nails down at the display case. Her lips were moving, probably giving a speech about organic ingredients, but Clara was losing. The kid already half-tasted our dessert. We had slipped it in his nose. Clara's sample spoons meant nothing to him now.

Because you just can't smell gelato.

About The Author

Sarah Haas has worked almost every kind of job there is. She shelved library books and managed a college dorm. She designed t-shirts and sawed metal signs. She taught high school English and directed plays. Her very first job was at McDonalds. The manager asked her only two questions at the interview, you know which ones. And yes, she failed both questions, but she started work there the next day.

As a kid, Sarah dreamed about traveling the world. She started studying Spanish in ninth grade. Now, she is about to move to the jungle of Peru. Her newest job? You could call it being a missionary. You could call it farming or paddling a canoe. Whatever kind of job she chooses, she will always keep writing new stories about the Spanish language and the people it leads her to.

Refried Dreams

About The Publisher

Story Shares is a nonprofit focused on supporting the millions of teens and adults who struggle with reading by creating a new shelf in the library specifically for them. The ever-growing collection features content that is compelling and culturally relevant for teens and adults, yet still readable at a range of lower reading levels.

Story Shares generates content by engaging deeply with writers, bringing together a community to create this new kind of book. With more intriguing and approachable stories to choose from, the teens and adults who have fallen behind are improving their skills and beginning to discover the joy of reading. For more information, visit storyshares.org.

Easy to Read. Hard to Put Down.

Made in the USA
Middletown, DE
20 January 2023

22687050R00043